A Terrible Thing Happened

Published by
MAGINATION PRESS
An Educational Publishing Foundation Book
American Psychological Association
750 First Street, NE
Washington, DC 20002

For more information about our books, including a complete catalog, please write to us, call 1-800-374-2721, or visit our website at www.maginationpress.com

Printed by Phoenix Color, Rockaway, New Jersey

Library of Congress Cataloging-in-Publication Data
Holmes, Margaret M., 1944-
A terrible thing happened / by Margaret M. Holmes ; afterword by Sasha J. Mudlaff ; illustrated by Cary Pillo.
p. cm.
Summary: After Sherman sees something terrible happen, he becomes anxious and then angry, but when a caring adult helps him talk about these emotions he feels better.
ISBN 1-55798-642-8 (hardcover).—ISBN 1-55798-701-7 (paperback).
[1. Emotional problems—Fiction.]
I. Mudlaff, Sasha J., 1967-. II. Pillo, Cary, ill. III. Title.

PZ7.H7364 Te 2000
[E]—dc21   99-040060

Manufactured in the United States of America
15 14 13 12 11

A Terrible Thing Happened

WRITTEN BY Margaret M. Holmes

ILLUSTRATED BY Cary Pillo

AFTERWORD BY Sasha J. Mudlaff

MAGINATION PRESS • WASHINGTON, DC

To all children

who struggle with the aftermath of tragedy,

and to their dedicated caregivers

MMH

To Ruth Gould,

for her dedication to helping children

CP

Sherman Smith saw the most terrible thing. He was very upset. It really scared Sherman to see such a terrible thing.

Sherman did not like
feeling so afraid.
He did not want to
remember what
happened.   So Sherman
decided not to think about
the terrible thing he saw.

Sherman thought
that would make
him feel better.

At first the plan seemed to work.
Sherman woke up every morning.
He brushed his teeth and he went to school.

Sherman played with his friends.
He teased his sister and he walked his dog.

Everything seemed all right for a while.
But something inside of Sherman was starting to bother him.

Sherman had to play more, run faster, and sing louder
in order to forget the terrible thing he saw.

Other things started happening to Sherman, too. Sometimes he did not feel hungry.

Sometimes his stomach hurt or his head hurt.

Sometimes he felt sad,
but he did not know why.

Sometimes he was nervous
for no reason at all.

Sometimes he did not sleep very well.

Sometimes when he did sleep
he had very bad dreams.
The bad dreams scared Sherman.

All of these things made Sherman angry.
It seemed like Sherman was angry all the time.

Sherman started getting into trouble at school.
Sometimes he felt so angry that he did mean things.

Getting into trouble so often made Sherman feel bad.

Sherman
did not
understand
all of his
bad feelings.
He felt
confused.

Sometimes parents help children figure out their feelings.
Sometimes teachers or other grown-ups help.
That is how Sherman met Ms. Maple.

Ms. Maple helped Sherman think about his feelings.
She listened while Sherman talked to her.
They played while they talked.
Sherman did not feel as mixed up when he talked to Ms. Maple.

Once when Sherman and
Ms. Maple were coloring,
she told him to draw a
picture of how he felt when
he was angry.   This seemed
like a strange thing to draw,
but Sherman did it.

After that,
Sherman
drew lots of
pictures.
Pictures of
the pain in
his stomach.
Pictures of
the bad
dreams
he had.
Pictures
of the fear
he felt.

And at last, pictures of the terrible thing he saw.

Sherman and
Ms. Maple
talked about
the pictures.
He asked if
the terrible
thing he
saw was
his fault.
Sherman
said he
worried a lot
about that.

"No," Ms. Maple
told Sherman,
"it was not your fault."

Sherman told
Ms. Maple a lot
of things.
He told her
about the
bad dreams.
He told her
how scared
he felt.
It was all very
hard to do.
Ms. Maple was
proud that
Sherman was
trying to talk
about such
hard things.

Sherman found that it felt good to let his feelings out.
Feeling good helped Sherman feel stronger.
When Sherman felt stronger, he did not feel so angry.

Nothing can
change the
terrible thing
that Sherman
saw, but now
he does not
feel so mean.
He is not
so scared
or worried.
His stomach
does not hurt
as much.
And the bad
dreams hardly
ever happen.

28

Sherman Smith is feeling much better now.
He just thought you would want to know.

A Note to Parents and Caregivers

BY SASHA J. MUDLAFF

Witnesses to a violent or traumatic event are considered "secondary victims." Surprisingly, research indicates that a child who is a secondary victim is more likely to turn to violence in the future than a child who is a primary victim. However, when children are able to talk to caring adults and understand their feelings after witnessing a traumatic event, the likelihood that they will perpetuate violence in the future is reduced.

A Terrible Thing Happened can thus be used to help open the channels of communication with a child who has witnessed any "terrible thing," including:

- accidents of any kind, such as a vehicle crash, an electrocution, or a fall
- assault
- school violence
- domestic violence
- gang violence
- situations of abuse, including substance abuse
- death
- homicide
- suicide
- natural disasters, such as a tornado, hurricane, or flood
- fire
- acts of war or their aftermath

Parents and other caregivers are often unsure of how to work with a child who has been traumatized by such events. These suggestions may be helpful.

1. This may be the child's first experience of having his or her basic belief system questioned. Such children's sense of security and safety has been threatened, which cannot help but change their view of the world. This is a very real loss for a child and should be viewed as an experience that causes grief, much like the death of someone they love.

2. Use words that are both real and accurate, and avoid euphemisms. Substitute words and phrases, although seemingly comforting to adults, can add to the child's confusion about what it is that he or she witnessed.

3. The child may be too terrified to even speak of the event for fear of repercussions or other reasons. Help to create a safe place for him or her to eventually tell the story and express the resulting feelings.

4. Give the child several modes for describing or acting out the event. Dolls, drawing materials, paint, crayons, sand, clay, puppets, stuffed animals, and other appropriate toys can all be used.

5. Recurring nightmares are very common. The more the child is able to safely "tell the story," the more these will diminish.

30

Keep in mind that different types of trauma will result in different issues for each child. For example, if the trauma was a car accident, a fear of riding in a car may develop. If the event was gang violence, the child may not want to go outdoors. Domestic violence may result in problematic issues of trust or, more seriously, attachment disorders.

Guilt and a sense of responsibility are normal reactions when children witness violence or trauma. Help the child to understand that the event was not his or her fault. Children's minds are often plagued with the "if only's," much as adults' are.

Children who have witnessed violence or trauma can experience fear, guilt, denial, anger, rage, confusion, desire for revenge, and loneliness, in any combination. In this story, Sherman internalizes his feelings, which turn into constant pangs of anger that are exhibited by his getting into trouble at school and doing mean things. He doesn't want to do these things, but he feels like he can't help himself. Watch for signs indicating that the child is struggling with any of these feelings.

Be aware that when internalizing fear and other feelings, the child can also be physically affected. In this story, for example, Sherman experiences loss of appetite, headaches, stomachaches, and sleeplessness.

Some children, particularly girls, may react to witnessing violence or trauma by becoming more quiet, withdrawn, or introverted. Their suffering is more likely to go unnoticed or unaddressed. Be watchful, and be prepared to offer special attention to help them express themselves, whether through play, art, or talking to a caring adult.

Attempt to maintain the child's daily routine as much as possible. This continuity helps provide the child with some sense of security and stability during a time full of uncertainty.

Maintaining rules and expectations is very important for rebuilding the child's feelings of security. Continue to expect the child to abide by the household and classroom rules even as he or she is working through this experience.

The child may already feel very different from others because of this experience; his or her self-esteem could, in fact, be greatly diminished. It is important that the child not be singled out for special privileges or compensations. He or she needs to feel a part of the peer group and should be expected to function accordingly.

Be prepared to listen well with your ears, eyes, and heart to what your child has to teach you about his or her grief.

Consider having the child meet with a professional, if even for one session, to rule out the need for formal therapy.

Helpful Resources

Aub, Kathleen. *Children Are Survivors Too: A Guidebook for Young Homicide Survivors.* Boca Raton, FL: Grief Education Enterprises, 1995. Twelve personal stories from children who are survivors or witnesses of violent deaths.

Barrett, R.K. "Children and Traumatic Loss." In K. Doka's (Ed.), *Children Mourning, Mourning Children* (pp. 85-88). Washington, DC: Taylor & Francis, 1995.

Bernstein, Sharon. *A Family That Fights.* Morton Grove, IL: Albert Whitman, 1991. Suggests words for children and parents to openly discuss domestic violence.

Berry, J. *About Traumatic Experiences.* Chicago: Children's Press, 1990. Answers to kids' questions about trauma and traumatic experiences (ages 8-11).

Cohen, Janice. *Why Did It Happen?* New York: Morrow Junior Books, 1994. In this book to help children cope with a violent world, Daniel witnesses a violent crime in the neighborhood and discusses how he feels about it.

Davis, D. *Something Is Wrong in My House.* Seattle, WA: Parenting Press, 1984. A book about parents fighting, ways to cope with violence, and how to break the cycle (ages 8-12).

Goldman, Linda. *Breaking the Silence: A Guide to Help Children With Complicated Grief: Suicide, Homicide, AIDS, Violence and Abuse.* Washington, DC: Accelerated Development, 1996.

Hendricks, Jean, et al. *When Father Kills Mother: Guiding Children Through Grief.* New York: Routledge, 1995.

Henry-Jenkins, Wanda. *Just Us.* Omaha, NE: Centering Corporation, 1993. For teenagers and young adults to help them understand and overcome homicidal loss and grief.

Kuklin, S. *After a Suicide: Young People Speak Up.* New York: G.P. Putnam's Sons, 1994. For young people who are survivors after a parent suicide.

Loftis, Chris. *The Boy Who Sat By the Window: Helping Children Cope With Violence.* Far Hills, NJ: New Horizon Press, 1996. Explores Joshua's reactions to the death of his friend by a random drive-by-shooting.

Loftis, Chris. *The Words Hurt.* Far Hills, NJ: New Horizon Press, 1995. A story for young children explaining how words can be hurtful and abusive and what children can do about it.

Mahon, K.L. *Just One Tear.* New York: Lothrop, Lee, and Shepard Books, 1992. The diary of a 13-year-old who witnesses his father being shot and fatally wounded.

Monahon, Cynthia. *Children and Trauma: A Guide for Parents and Professionals.* San Francisco: Jossey-Bass, 1997. Teaches parents and others who care for children about what they can do to understand and ameliorate the effects of trauma on children.

Salloum, Alison. *Reactions.* Omaha, NE: Centering Corporation, 1998. Intended to help children and youth understand grief and how trauma affects them physically and emotionally.

Schleifer, Jay. *Everything You Need to Know When Someone You Know Has Been Killed.* New York: Rosen Publishing Group, 1998. Speaks directly to youth suffering traumatic loss.

Smith, I. (Ed.). *We Don't Like Remembering Them as a Field of Grass.* Portland, OR: The Dougy Center, 1991. A book by children of many ages telling how they feel about the murder of a loved one (ages 7-16).

Sasha J. Mudlaff, M.A., is a children's grief counselor and the Director of Hamilton's Academy of Grief and Loss in Des Moines, Iowa.